For Mama
and her two Ninjas

with love from Papa

Copyright © Niki Daly 1992

The right of Niki Daly to be identified as the author and
illustrator of this work has been asserted by him in
accordance with the Copyright, Designs and Patents Act, 1988

First published in 1992 by The Bodley Head Children's Books
an imprint of The Random Century Group Ltd
20 Vauxhall Bridge Road, London SW1V 2SA

Printed in Hong Kong

A CIP catalogue record of this book is
available from the British Library

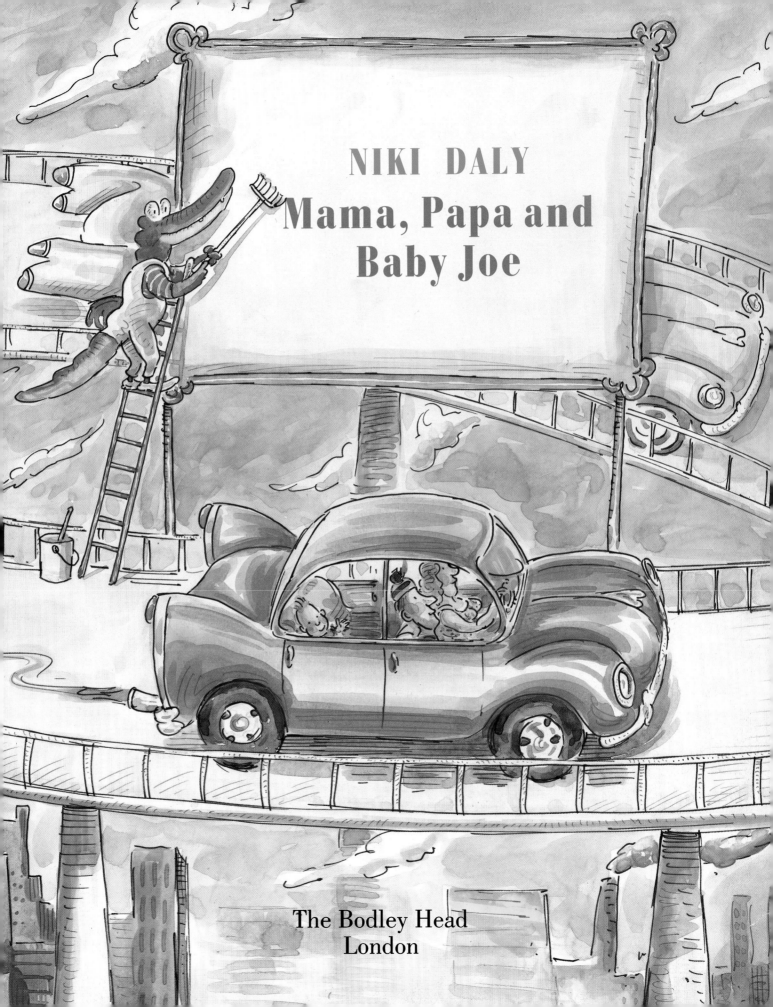

NIKI DALY
Mama, Papa and Baby Joe

The Bodley Head
London

Under over Coca-Cola
Off to Pick 'n' Pay we go,

Moany moany macaroni,
Mama, Papa, and Baby Joe.

Harum-scarum through the traffic

Ziggery-zaggery park the car.

Bumpity-bump along the pavement

Around the block and there you are!

In and out the shops so busy
Mama and Papa go yakety-yak.

See you later, escalator
Okeydokey, clickety-clack.

Pushalong singalong, shopping trolley
Chicken Lickin and Pudding Pack,

Oozy-poozy tube of toothpaste
Squeezy fingers, smackety-smack!

Hubbly-bubbly King Kong Cola
Spaghetti falling pitter-pat,

Hot and bothered screaming Mama

"DON'T DO THAT!"

"DON'T DO THAT!"

Checkout lady checks the shopping
Money honey jingle jam,

Papa, Mama in a tizzy
Boogie-woogie in the pram!

Up and down the elevator
Hickory-dickory acrobat,

Hot and bothered fussing Papa

"YOU CAN'T HAVE THAT!"

"YOU CAN'T HAVE THAT!"

Sitting sipping King Kong Cola
In Fatty Boom Boom's Take Away,

Sticky icky licking baby
Mama smiling, it's OK!

Baby needs to do a pee-pee

Quickero backero tiddly-pom,

Button up all the pretty blue buttons
Billy 'n' Barney, Sally 'n' Tom.

Under over Coca-Cola
Shopping packed and home we go!
Honky-tonky through the city
Mama, Papa, and sleepy Joe.